This Book is Dedicated to
Yvonne Fedderson & Sara O'Meara
founders of Childhelp U.S.A. and also to the volunteers of
The San Diego Chapter of Childhelp U.S.A.
for all their selfless effort to raise money to fight child abuse.

Copyright © 2001 by Timothy Anders.
Published by Alpine Publishing, Inc.
1119 S. Mission Rd., PMB 102
Fallbrook, CA 92028

Printed in China.
Graphic Art by Dr. Hope. Translation by Ruth Conrique.

Library of Congress Catalog Number: 00-109265

LAUGHING DAY / EL DÍA PARA REÍR by Dr. Hope, J.A.P.D.

Summary: A young lad learns a valuable lesson which he teaches to others. Written in both English and Spanish.
1. Bilingual—Fiction. 2. English-Spanish—Fiction. 3. Fairy Tales—Fiction. 4. Nursery Rhymes—Fiction. 5. Stories in Rhyme—Fiction. I. Title.

00-109265
ISBN 1-88562-60-3
1 3 5 7 9 10 8 6 4 2
FIRST IMPRESSION

Laughing Day

El Día para Reír

in English & Spanish - en íngles y español

written by **Dr. Hope, J.A.P.D.**

(**J**ust **A** **P**retend **D**octor)

illustrated by **Dan Hamilton**

No Gronks or Pickled Palamadora were injured in the making of this storybook.

In the Great Valley, the valley so wide,
lived the Boologs and Grumpies on each forest side.

On the side of the Boologs lived a lad and his mother,
Oolong, the lad, and his one younger brother.

His mother sent Oolong to the marketplace,
a big ol' smile upon his face.

A diferentes lados del bosque en el Gran Valle
vivían los Bulogs y los Gruñones en el ancho valle.

Al lado de los Bulogs, vivían la mamá y sus dos hijitos,
Ulong era el mayor de los dos hermanitos.

Su mamá mandó a Ulong al mercado,
iba con una sonrisa en su cara de lado a lado.

He said to Abaloo, I heard him say,
"It's almost time for Laughing Day."

Abaloo, the storekeeper, went on to say,
"Can I help you with something, if I may?"

"My mother has told me that I must buy
some Pickled Palamadora," he did reply.

Pickled Palamadora, the delicacy of the land
is so delicious even when canned.

Le dijo a Abalú, yo lo escuché decir:
"Ya casi llega El Día Para Reír".

A Abalú el tendero, entonces se le oyó decir:
"¿Hay algo en lo que te pueda servir?"

"Mi madre me ha dicho que debo comprar
Palamadora en Vinagre", dijo al contestar.

Palamadora en Vinagre, de la comarca el manjar,
tan delicioso aun cuando embotada llega a estar.

"Alas young lad, it's been gone for a week
the Pickled Palamadora which you seek.

There's none to be found, not even spillage;
you'll have to travel to the Grumpies' village.

The Grumpies are disagreeable and mean,
they're the rudest people I've ever seen.

But Pickled Palamadora, there surely will be
for they don't celebrate with this delicacy."

"Lo siento niño, no hemos tenido por una semana -
la Palamadora en Vinagre que buscas esta mañana.

No tenemos nada, ni siquiera lo derramado
tendrás que viajar a los Gruñones al otro lado.

Los Gruñones son desagradables y malos,
en el mundo son los más mal educados.

Pero Palamadora en Vinagre seguramente habrá,
porque ellos no celebran con ese manjar".

"They don't celebrate anything at all
and never go to the Laughing Day Ball.

But I must ask, young lad, if you go
a favor for me, something I need so.

My shelves are all empty, but I think if you try,
some Pickled Palamadora for me you could buy."

Abaloo thought, 'cause he had a hunch,
the lad could not carry a very big bunch.

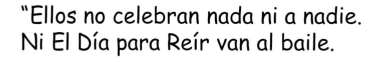

"Ellos no celebran nada ni a nadie.
Ni El Día para Reír van al baile.

Pero debo pedirte niño, si es que vas,
algo que necesito, que un favor me hagas.

Mis alacenas están vacías, pero si logras llegar,
Palamadora en Vinagre para mi podrías comprar".

Abalú pensó porque se le ocurrió al pensar,
que el niño una gran cantidad no podría cargar.

"But you must be careful and return by tomorrow;
on these conditions, the cart you may borrow."

So into the Dark Forest went Oolong that day,
pushing the cart through this treacherous way.

The forest was dense, which cut off the light,
it was almost as if he was traveling by night.

Oolong felt nervous but this way he was bound,
toward the village of the Grumpies, the very next town.

Pero tienes que tener cuidado y para mañana regresar;
bajo estas condiciones, el carrito te puedo prestar".

Así es que Ulong entró al Bosque Obscuro ese día,
empujando el carrito por esa traidora vía.

El bosque estaba tan espeso que la luz cortaba,
era casi como que en la noche viajaba.

Ulong se sentía nervioso, pero ese era el camino
a la aldea de los Gruñones, la cual era su destino.

Because of his fear, he went fast, not slow;
he tripped on a rock and down he did go.

The cart went on, aimed toward a tree,
and then a loud crash came suddenly.

He looked toward the source of the sound
and saw the cart's wheel; it lay on the ground.

Oolong sat down where the wheel did lie;
he felt so bad that he began to cry.

Porque tenía miedo, muy rápido viajó,
se tropezó en una piedra y al suelo cayó.

El carrito hacia un árbol siguió al frente,
y un gran choque se escuchó de repente.

Entonces él vio de donde el ruido venía,
y vio que la rueda del carrito en el suelo yacía.

A donde estaba la rueda Ulong se fue a sentar,
pues se sentía tan mal que se puso a llorar.

"Why do you cry?" he heard someone say.
He saw an old man whose hair was all gray.

Startled a bit from the words that were spoken,
Oolong replied, "My cart has been broken!"

"Well young lad, we'll use these two sticks;
we'll use them as levers and the cart we will fix."

The use of the levers made the cart like a feather
and soon they were done, for they worked well together.

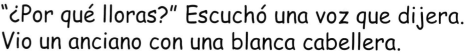

"¿Por qué lloras?" Escuchó una voz que dijera.
Vio un anciano con una blanca cabellera.

Sorprendido un poco por las palabras que habló,
Ulong le contestó: "Mi carrito se quebró".

"Bueno niño, estos dos palos usaremos;
y juntos el carrito arreglaremos".

Usando los palos el carrito levantaron,
pronto terminaron, porque juntos trabajaron.

"How can I repay you for your kindness and help?
Thank you, thank you!" Oolong said with a yelp.

"Just one thing I ask," said the man with a glow,
"Spread kindness and be helpful, wherever you go.

Should you encounter someone in need,
into their heart plant this gentle seed.

Help one another without thought of pay,
and to those who listen, repeat what I say."

"¿Como le puedo pagar por su amabilidad y su ayuda?
¡Gracias, gracias!," dijo Ulong con voz aguda.

"Solo te pido una cosa", él dijo con un brillo en sus ojos
"Amabilidad debes esparcir, como si fueran despojos.

Si te encuentras alguien que lo necesita,
en su corazón siembra esta gentil semillita.

Ayúdense unos a los otros sin pensar en pago,
y a los que escuchan, repíteles lo que yo hago".

So off Oolong went, not fast and not slow,
pushing the cart, his heart all aglow.

He entered the village, the road was quite bumpy;
soon Oolong would meet his very first Grumpy.

Oolong asked a Grumpy, coming through a door,
if he would direct him to the Palamadora store.

The Grumpy just walked away, (what a rude little elf);
when asked again, he said, "Go find it yourself!"

Así es que Ulong siguió, ni rápido ni despacito,
con su corazón encendido, empujando el carrito.

Entró a la aldea, el camino bastante irregular.
Pronto con su primer Gruñón, Ulong se iba a encontrar.

Ulong le preguntó a un Gruñón que por una puerta salía,
si la ubicación de una tienda de Palamadora sabía.

El malo Gruñón sin contestar se fue caminando
Finalmente él dijo: "A ver si tu solo la vas buscando".

Oolong then pushed his cart down the street,
and there an old woman he happened to meet.

Her bag had broken and spilled in the clover
and to pick up her stuff, she had to bend over.

She held her back as she bent over in pain
moaning and crying, her tears fell like rain.

Oolong went over to help the old elf.
"I've no money to pay you, I'll do it myself."

Ulong entonces por la calle su carrito empujó,
y ahí con una mujer anciana se encontró.

Su bolsa se rompió y todo por el pasto cayó,
y para recoger sus cosas, hacia abajo se agachó.

Se agarró de la espalda con dolor agachándose,
sus lagrimas corrían como ríos, llorando y quejándose.

Ulong se acercó a la vieja duende para ayudar.
"Yo lo hago sola" dijo, "No tengo dinero para pagar".

"Oh let me help you," Oolong went on to say,
"I'll help you for nothing, there's nothing to pay."

He picked up her stuff, it took a short while
he helped her home on her face was a smile.

"I've never said thank you before this day;
I wish there was something to you I could pay."

Ulong le dijo: "Permítame ayudar".
"Le ayudo por nada, no hay nada que pagar".

Recogió él de la anciana sus cosas, un rato tardó.
Le ayudó hasta su casa — en su cara una sonrisa se vio.

"Nunca he dicho gracias antes de este día;
que te pudiera pagar algo, yo desearía".

"Just one thing I ask," he said all aglow,
"Spread kindness and be helpful wherever you go.

Should you encounter someone in need,
into their heart plant this gentle seed.

Help one another without thought of pay,
and to those who listen, repeat what I say."

"Solo una cosa pido", dijo él con el rostro brillante,
"Amabilidad y ayuda esparza, de aquí en adelante.

Si se encuentra con alguien que lo necesita,
en su corazón siembre esta gentil semillita.

Ayúdense unos a los otros sin pensar en pago,
y a los que escuchen, repítales lo que hago".

She thought for a moment then said that she would;
she knew in her heart that it would feel good.

Oolong said good-bye and in a spirit of laughter,
told her it was Pickled Palamadora he was after.

She gave him directions as best as she could,
and thanked him again for his spirit of good.

Lo pensó un momento y luego dijo que lo haría;
sabía en su corazón que bien se sentiría.

En espíritu de risa Ulong se despidió muy alegre,
y le dijo que lo que buscaba era Palamadora en Vinagre.

Como mejor pudo, le dio ella instrucciones de verdad,
y de nuevo le dio gracias por su espíritu de bondad.

To the store Oolong went as quick as a horse;
he bought Pickled Palamadora and started home, of course.

But before he could leave this grumpy old town
he encountered an elf with his hands on the ground.

"What is the problem?" Oolong began to say.
"I've lost my Gronk. You can just go away!"

As you may know, a Gronk makes no sound,
but Oolong could see one: the Gronk had been found.

A la tienda fue Ulong, tan rápido como su paso le permitió,
compró Palamadora en Vinagre y a su casa se dirigió.

Cuando de la aldea de los Gruñones salía,
se encontró un duende que las manos en el piso tenía.

"¿Cual es el problema?" Ulong empezó a decir.
Dijo el duende, "Perdí mi Gronk, y tu ya te puedes ir".

Como tu lo sabes, un Gronk no hace ruido,
pero Ulong podía ver uno, el Gronk encontrado había sido.

He picked up the Gronk, gave it back to the elf.
The elf said, "Hrrumph, what do you want for yourself?"

Oolong said, "Nothing, just have a nice day."
The elf couldn't believe there was nothing to pay.

The elf felt something, to him strange and weird;
for the first time in his life a smile appeared.

"May I do something for you, some sort of task?
I'll do anything, you just have to ask."

Ulong levantó al Gronk y se lo entregó al duende así.
El duende dijo gruñendo, "¿Que es lo que quieres para ti?"

Ulong le dijo que solo le deseaba un buen día pasar.
El duende no podía creer, que no había nada que pagar.

El duende sintió algo que para él era extraño sentir.
Por primera vez en su vida sintió que quería reír.

"¿Puedo hacer alguna cosa por ti?
Haré cualquier cosa, solo tienes que pedir".

"Just one thing I ask," Oolong said with a glow,
"Spread kindness and be helpful wherever you go.

Should you encounter someone in need,
into their heart plant this gentle seed.

Help one another without thought of pay,
and to those who listen, repeat what I say."

"Solo una cosa pido", dijo Ulong con rostro brillante,
"Amabilidad y ayuda esparza, de aquí en adelante.

Si se encuentra con alguien que lo necesita,
en su corazón siembre esta gentil semillita.

Ayúdense los unos a los otros sin pensar en pago,
y a los que escuchen, repítales lo que yo hago".

The elf thought for a moment, then said that he would,
for he knew in his heart that it would feel good.

So Oolong returned, through the forest so deep,
a little bit tired and wanting to sleep.

He went to the store and yelled, "Abaloo!
The Pickled Palamadora, I've brought it for you."

When he told his mother the adventures he'd had,
she put him to bed, saying, "You're a good lad."

El duende pensó y luego dijo que lo haría,
porque en su corazón sabía que bien se sentiría.

Ulong se regresó por el bosque espeso,
queriendo dormir y todo eso.

Fue a la tienda y a Abalú le gritó:
"Le traje las cosas que usted me pidió".

Cuando lo que paso a su madre le dijo,
lo acostó en la cama dicendo: "Eres buen hijo".

But then two weeks later, I must say,
something strange happened on Laughing Day.

Pickled Palamadora was flowing free.
There was plenty to share for you and me.

Then all of a sudden there came a delegation,
an unexpected group to join the celebration.

They were playing and laughing with smiles well lit;
it was the Grumpies, though their name no longer fit.

Each one Oolong helped, had helped two others.
New friendships had grown; they all felt like brothers.

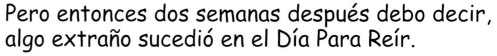

Pero entonces dos semanas después debo decir,
algo extraño sucedió en el Día Para Reír.

Palamadora en Vinagre que fluía yo vi.
Había bastante para compartir para ti y para mí.

Pues de repente un grupo grande llegó,
un grupo inesperado que a la celebración se unió.

Era un grupo de Gruñones que sonreía y jugaba,
aunque su nombre ya no les quedaba.

Cada uno que Ulong ayudó, ayudó a dos más.
Se sintieron como hermanos nuevos y mucho más.

The two turned to four, the four turned to eight.
The next thing they knew, there was no one to hate.

So to better the world, here is the way
remember this lesson from Laughing Day.

Just one thing to do, I think you now know:
Spread kindness and be helpful wherever you go.

Should you encounter someone in need,
into their heart plant this gentle seed.

Help one another without thought of pay,
and to those who listen, repeat what I say.

Dos se hicieron cuatro como al multiplicar.
Y en un rato ya no hubo más a quien odiar.

Para mejorar el mundo, si quieres ponerlo en acción —
del Día Para Reír recuerda la lección.

Solo una cosa ya sabes que debes hacer;
Amabilidad y ayuda esparcir por doquier.

Si encuentras alguien que lo necesita,
en sus corazones siembra esta gentil semillita.

Ayúdense los unos a los otros sin pensar en pago,
y a los que escuchen, repíteles lo que hago.

Author Dr. Hope wants you to know about

Childhelp USA®

a non-profit organization that tirelessly fights child abuse.
You can help too. If you suspect that a child is being neglected or abused,
please call the child abuse hotline at:

1 800 4 A CHILD

They can help. On behalf of that child we thank you.

Other Books, Cassettes and CDs by Dr. Hope, J.A.P.D.

24 hr. Order Line: **800 549 7080**

Chip, the Little Computer (written in English and Spanish)

An award winning story about a little computer who learns the value of determination and having faith in his dream.

The Frog Who Couldn't Jump

Freddie the Frog learns that you don't have to come in first to be a winner.

Punctuation Pals

Punctuation made fun and easy with colors and cool art.

The Laughing Day CD (story in both English and Spanish)

The Laughing Day story is acted out by talented voice actors
along with five humorous original songs written and performed by Russ T. Nailz.

Chip, the Little Computer CD (story in both English and Spanish)

Chip, the Little Computer story is acted out by talented voice actors
along with five humorous original songs written and performed by Russ T. Nailz.

The Frog Who Couldn't Jump CD

The Frog Who Couldn't Jump story is acted out by talented voice actors
along with five humorous original songs written and performed by Russ T. Nailz.

Also available are: Punctuation Pals, The Frog Who Couldn't Jump,
Chip, the Little Computer and Laughing Day T-Shirts and coloring books.

Visit Dr. Hope's *FREE* Game & Music Website at:

www.laughingday.com